Can You Greet the Whole Wide World?

12 common phrases in 12 different languages

**To all the friends that have blessed
my life—with love and thanks for
making the journey more joyous!
—L.E.**

**For Kate and Charlotte
—D.R.**

**We would like to thank Berlitz
for all their assistance on this book.**

Text copyright © 2006 by Lezlie Evans
Illustrations copyright © 2006 by Denis Roche

www.houghtonmifflinbooks.com

The text of this book is set in Agenda.
The illustrations are gouache.

Library of Congress Cataloging-in-Publication Data
Evans, Lezlie. Can you greet the whole wide world? : 12 common phrases in 12
different languages / by Lezlie Evans ; illustrated by Denis Roche.
p. cm.
ISBN 0-618-56327-X (hardcover : alk. paper)
1. Salutations—Juvenile literature. I. Roche, Denis. II. Title.
GT3050.E83 2006
395.4—dc22
2005020612

ISBN-13: 978-0618-56327-2

Printed in China
SCP 10 9 8 7 6 5 4 3 2 1

Can You Greet the Whole Wide World?

12 common phrases in 12 different languages

by Lezlie Evans

illustrated by Denis Roche

Houghton Mifflin Company

Boston 2006

Kids throughout this great big world
are very much like you.
They like to read and laugh and play,
and do the things you do.

So learn to greet the whole wide world—
quite soon you'll see it's true.
Now, don't be shy, go on, speak up
and make a friend or two.

The sun is up, it's morning time.
Hooray! School starts today.
Try calling out, *"**Good morning**"*
to your friends along the way.

*guten Morgen	(gooten morgan)	German
boker tov	(BO-kehr tove)	Hebrew
buenos días	(bwen-os dee-us)	Spanish
sab'a alkair	(sah-bah al-care)	Arabic
dobroye utro	(doe-broyeh oo-tra)	Russian
shubh probhaat	(shoe-bah prah-BOT)	Hindi
dzau an	(zow on)	Chinese
sawubona	(sow-oo bone-uh)	Zulu
ohayo gozaimasu	(oh-HI-oh go-zie-moss)	Japanese
buon giorno	(bwon JOR-no)	Italian
bonjour	(bohn-zhure)	French
bom dia	(boam jee-ah)	Portuguese

You head into your classroom.
Your friends all say **_hello_**.
While hanging up your book bag,
greet everyone you know.

guten Tag	**(gooten tog)**	German
shalom	**(shah-lome)**	Hebrew
hola	**(OH-la)**	Spanish
ahalan	**(ah-lan)**	Arabic
privet	**(priv-YET)**	Russian
namaste'	**(nam-us-steh)**	Hindi
ni-hao	**(NEE-how)**	Chinese
yebo	**(YEH-bo)**	Zulu
konnichiwa	**(kon-nee-chee-wah)**	Japanese
ciao	**(chow)**	Italian
salut	**(sah-lue)**	French
ola	**(oh-la)**	Portuguese

When meeting this year's teacher,
you're not sure what to say.
Surprise her and ask, *"How are you?"*
in a new and different way.

Wie geht's?	**(vee-gates?)**	German
Ma shlomech?	**(mah shlo-mehck?)**	Hebrew
¿Cómo está?	**(komo ess-sta?)**	Spanish
Kaifa halok?	**(kay-fa ha-look?)**	Arabic
Kak dyela?	**(kock de-LA?)**	Russian
Aap kaise hai?	**(ahp keh-sah hain?)**	Hindi
Ni hao ma?	**(nee-how-ma?)**	Chinese
Ninjani?	**(nin-JARn-nee?)**	Zulu
O genki deesu ka?	**(oh gen-kee des-kah?)**	Japanese
Come stai?	**(ko-may sta?)**	Italian
Comment ça va?	**(komo sa vah?)**	French
Como vai?	**(komo vie?)**	Portuguese

You sit down by the new kid.
It's time for show-and-tell.
So go on, ask him, *"What's your name?"*
Then share your name as well.

Wie heißen Sie?	**(vee hi-sen zee?)**	German
Ma shmech?	**(ma shim-ehck?)**	Hebrew
¿Cómo se llama usted?	**(como seh-yahmah oo-sted?)**	Spanish
*Ma ismok?	**(maa is-moke?)**	Arabic
Kock vas zovut?	**(kock vaz zo-voot?)**	Russian
Aapka naam kya hai?	**(ahp-ka nam kya hay?)**	Hindi
Ni jiao shen me ming zi?	**(nee jow shen mah ming zih?)**	Chinese
Igama lakho ungubani?	**(ee-ga-ma la-ko goo-bah-knee?)**	Zulu
Namie wah nani?	**(nam-eye wah nan-ee?)**	Japanese
Come ti chiami?	**(ko-may tee kee-ahm-ee?)**	Italian
Comment tu t'appelles?	**(komo too ta-pel?)**	French
Como voce se chama?	**(komo vohs-sey see shah-ma?)**	Portuguese

In Math your neighbor asks you,
"Do you understand?"
You answer, *"No,"* and then get help
when you raise your hand.

nein	(nine)	German
lo	(low)	Hebrew
no	(no)	Spanish
laa	(lah)	Arabic
* nyet	(nyet)	Russian
nahin	(nuh-he)	Hindi
bu-shi	(boo-shih)	Chinese
cha	(kah)	Zulu
iie	(ee-yeh)	Japanese
no	(no)	Italian
non	(no)	French
não	(now[n])	Portuguese

It's time for lunch! You wait in line
so you can pick and choose.
When offered something yummy,
please is the word to use.

bitte	(BIT-teh)	German
bevakasha	(be-vaka-SHAW)	Hebrew
por favor	(pour fah-vor)	Spanish
min fadilak	(min fod-lick)	Arabic
phazhaluista	(paw-ZHA-loo-sta)	Russian
kRipayaa	(kripay-uh)	Hindi
qing	(ching)	Chinese
uxolo	(ook-kolo)	Zulu
kudasai	(koo-dah-sie)	Japanese
per favore	(pair fa-VOAR-ay)	Italian
s'il vous plaît	(seal-vu-play)	French
por favor	(pour fa-vor)	Portuguese

You start a game at recess.
A new friend wants to play.
By saying, **"Yes,** come on, join in,"
you're sure to make her day!

ja	(jah)	German
ken	(kehn)	Hebrew
sí	(see)	Spanish
na'am	(na-ahm)	Arabic
da	(daw)	Russian
ha	(huh[n])	Hindi
*shi	(shih)	Chinese
yebo	(YEAH-bo)	Zulu
hai	(hi)	Japanese
sì	(see)	Italian
oui	(wee)	French
sim	(seen[g])	Portuguese

While walking through the hallway,
you accidentally slip.
I'm sorry is the phrase you'll use
when those behind you trip.

entschuldigung	**(ent-SHOOL-di-goong)**	German
slach li	**(slohck lee)**	Hebrew
lo siento	**(low see-en-toe)**	Spanish
aasif	**(a-ah-seef)**	Arabic
izvinite	**(ease-vee-nee-tyeh)**	Russian
shamma kare	**(shah-MAH kah-ray)**	Hindi
dui bu qi	**(do-ee boo chee)**	Chinese
*uxolo	**(ook-kolo)**	Zulu
gomen ne	**(go-men neh)**	Japanese
scusami	**(skoo-za-me)**	Italian
pardon	**(pahr-doe[n])**	French
desculpe-me	**(des-scoop-i-me)**	Portuguese

Your hefty stack of library books
is way too much for you.
Say *thank you* to your friend who helps,
and thank the librarian too!

danke	**(DUNG-keh)**	German
to'dV	**(toe-DAH)**	Hebrew
gracias	**(GRAH-see-us)**	Spanish
shokran	**(shoke-run)**	Arabic
spasibo	**(spahseebah)**	Russian
dhanya-waad	**(d-hun-vahd)**	Hindi
xie-xie	**(sheh-sheh)**	Chinese
ngiyabonga	**([n]kee-AH-bone-ga)**	Zulu
*arigato	**(ah-ree-gah-toe)**	Japanese
grazie	**(GRAT-zee-ay)**	Italian
merci	**(mair-see)**	French
obrigado	**(oh-bree-gah-doe)**	Portuguese

Come on, let's line up for the bus.
Please gather up your things.
Then say **goodbye** to all your friends
before the school bell rings.

auf Wiedersehen	**(owf VEE-der-zain)**	German
lehitraot	**(leh-hit-rah-oat)**	Hebrew
adiós	**(ah-dee-OHS)**	Spanish
Ma'a Salama	**(ma-ah sah-lah-mah)**	Arabic
dO svidanja	**(daw svee-don-ya)**	Russian
phir melenge	**(phir me-leng-gay)**	Hindi
zai-jian	**(zie-jen)**	Chinese
sizobonana	**(sees-oh-bo-NON-NA)**	Zulu
sayonara	**(sigh-yo-nah-ra)**	Japanese
arrivederci	**(a-ree-veh-DARE-chee)**	Italian
au revoir	**(oh-reh-VWAh[r])**	French
adeus	**(ah-day-ohs)**	Portuguese

When you come through the door from school,
the first thing that you do
is share a hug with those at home
and tell them, *"I love you!"*

Ich liebe dich!	**(ikh lee-beh dikh)**	German
Ani ohevet otakh!	**(a-NEE o-HAYV o-TAHK)**	Hebrew
Te amo!	**(tay-ahmo)**	Spanish
Ohepok!	**(oh-heh-pohk)**	Arabic
Ya tyebya lyublyu!	**(yah teh-bya loo-bloo)**	Russian
Mein Tumse Pyar Karta Hoon!	**(me-in toom-see pee-are kar-thah hoon)**	Hindi
Wo ai ni!	**(woh eye nee)**	Chinese
Ngiyakuthanda!	**([n]gee-yah-koo-tahn-da)**	Zulu
Daisuki!	**(dye-skee)**	Japanese
Ti amo!	**(tee ahmo)**	Italian
Je t'aime!	**(zher tem)**	French
Eu te amo!	**(eh-oo chee ah-mo)**	Portuguese

At last your day is over
and Dad turns out the light.
As Mom bends down for one last kiss,
how do you say *good night*?

gute Nacht	(goo-teh nokht)	German
liala tov	(lie-la tove)	Hebrew
buenas noches	(bwen-ahs no-chess)	Spanish
laila tayyeba	(lie-la tah-yeba)	Arabic
spokoinoi nochi	(spa-koi-noi no-chee)	Russian
shubha raatri	(shoe-bah raw-tree)	Hindi
wan an	(wahn ahn)	Chinese
lala kahle	(la-la gah-sleh)	Zulu
oyasumi nasai	(oh-ya-su-me nah-sigh)	Japanese
buona notte	(boo-on-ah no-tay)	Italian
bonne nuit	(bohn new-ee)	French
*boa noite	(boa noiche)	Portuguese

**Now that you can greet the world,
would you like to see
where each tongue is spoken?
Come check it out with me!**

German:
1 Germany
2 Austria
3 Belgium

Hebrew:
4 Israel

Spanish:
5 Spain
6 Mexico
7 Colombia
8 Argentina
9 Chile
10 Cuba
11 Dominican Republic
12 Equatorial Guinea
13 Ecuador
14 Venezuela
15 Costa Rica
16 Nicaragua
17 Honduras
18 Guatemala
19 Panama
20 El Salvador
21 Peru
22 Bolivia
23 Paraguay
24 Uruguay

Arabic:
25 Algeria
26 Bahrain
27 Chad
28 Djibouti
29 Egypt
30 Eritrea
31 Iraq
32 Israel

33 Jordan
34 Kuwait
35 Lebanon
36 Libya
37 Mauritania
38 Morocco
39 Oman
40 Qatar
41 Saudi Arabia
42 Sudan
43 Syria
44 United Arab Emirates
45 Tunisia
46 Yemen

Russian:
47 Russia
48 Belarus
49 Kazakhstan
50 Kyrgyzstan
51 Turkmenistan
52 Tajikistan
53 Uzbekistan

Hindi:
54 India

Chinese:
55 China
56 Singapore
57 Taiwan
58 Hong Kong

Zulu:
59 South Africa

Japanese:
60 Japan

Italian:
61 Italy

French:
62 France
63 Belgium
64 Canada
65 Haiti
66 Monaco
67 Benin
68 Burkina Faso
69 Burundi
70 Cameroon
71 Central African Republic
72 Chad
73 Congo
74 Côte d'Ivoire
75 Djibouti
76 Gabon
77 Guinea
78 Luxembourg
79 Madagascar
80 Mauritania
81 Niger
82 Rwanda
83 Senegal
84 Togo
85 Democratic Republic of Congo

Portuguese:
86 Portugal
87 Angola
88 Brazil
89 Cape Verde
90 East Timor
91 Mozambique

Here are some of the countries in which these languages are officially spoken.

THE END

El fin

La fin

L'estremita

O fim

Das Ende